Moon and Otter and Frog

MOON and OTTER and FROG

Laura Simms

Illustrated by Clifford Brycelea

Hyperion Books for Children / New York

To my loving children,
Daryl, Dyami, Reymond, and Amelia
— C. B.

For Vi, for May, and for Roberta,
shining moon torches in the night
— L. S.

Text © 1995 by Laura Simms.
Illustrations © 1995 by Clifford Brycelea.
All rights reserved.
Printed in Singapore.
For information address Hyperion Books for Children,
114 Fifth Avenue, New York, New York 10011.
FIRST EDITION
1 3 5 7 9 10 8 6 4 2

Library of Congress Cataloging-in-Publication Data
Simms, Laura
Moon and Otter and Frog/Laura Simms: illustrated by Clifford
Brycelea.
p. cm.
Summary: With the help of friend Otter, Moon finds a bride in
Little Ugly Green Frog, who lacks physical beauty but possesses a
special gift.
ISBN: 0-7868-0027-5 (trade) — ISBN 0-7868-2022-5 (lib. bdg.)
1. Modoc Indians — Legends. [1. Modoc Indians — Legends.
2. Indians of North America — Legends. 3. Moon — Folklore.]
I. Brycelea, Clifford, ill. II. Title.
E99.M7S46 1995
398.2'089974 — dc20
[E] 93-39879
CIP
AC

When I read a version of *Moon and Otter and Frog*, a tale of the Modoc tribe, as recorded by Jeremiah Curtin, an American writer who collected international folkore in the late nineteenth century, I fell in love with Ugly Green Frog, just as Moon did, for her gentleness and her power. I began retelling the story to children. Their intense and poignant response was my guide to keep exploring the depth and meaning in the story, and find out as much as I could about the Modoc people who told this tale.

The Modoc myths take place in that time before the world took shape as we know it, when everything was alive with spirit. As I told this tale, I could feel my and the children's imaginations and hearts expanding. I visited Klamath Lakes, where the Modoc lived before they were almost completely destroyed by war and illness in the 1850s. Sitting by the lakes, looking at a landscape of abundant water and greenery, I understood the less obvious teaching in the tale about the interdependence of everything, and the power of nature to re-plenish itself and the world and the heart. In British Columbia, I saw the face of a brown-skinned otter poke itself up out of the water, and was moved by its resemblance to a full moon. I began to delight in the friendship between Otter and the Moon come down as a warrior to Earth. I understood Moon's loneli-ness and the shyness of Ugly Frog.

Through the retelling of this story, I hope to inspire faith in children to trust their inner beauty. I also hope to honor the Modoc who lived here before my ancestors and increase respect for the wisdom and compassion imprinted in their stories. The strength of Native American stories waits ready to blossom, like a seed inside words, like Frog in the heart of Moon, for each one of us who listens, living between Earth and sky.

— Laura Simms

In the earliest times, when the world was still forming, the full moon lived alone in the night sky. The stars and the clouds had not yet appeared. Moon was lonely. Every night he stared at another full moon in the great waters below. "I wonder if he sees me," pondered Moon.

One evening clouds began to form. They moved across the sky in the shapes of animals. Moon hoped to make some friends. But the biggest clouds, the grizzly bear clouds, were jealous of Moon. They chewed on him to make him smaller. Moon grew sad and decided to go visit the other full moon that he saw every night.

Moon descended to the earth in the form of a young warrior wearing a white buckskin suit adorned with silver beads and white porcupine quills. He walked until he came to the edge of the great waters he had seen from the sky.

However, at the water's edge he discovered that what he had seen was not another moon like himself. It was Otter. Otter's white face shone in the night just like a full moon.

Otter was surprised also because he had thought that Moon was an otter in the sky. "I wondered about you. I asked myself two questions: What does that otter eat? Is there water in the sky?" said Otter as he nibbled on a piece of pink shrimp. Moon and Otter laughed and told each other about the earth and the sky.

Moon stayed on the earth. He and Otter became best friends. Otter, his wife, and their six children often tied themselves to rocks with seaweed and, lying on their backs munching sea urchins and crabs, chatted all day with Moon about the sky. At night Moon took his full, round sky form, casting a pool of white light for the children to play in. Moon was no longer lonely.

After a while, even though Moon loved his friend, he wanted to go back to the sky. He asked Otter to accompany him. But Otter couldn't leave his family. "Why don't you find a wife to go with you?" he suggested to Moon.

"Do you know any girls who would want to live in the sky?" asked Moon.

"I do," said Otter, setting a piece of fish on his belly while he talked. "On the other shore there are ten pretty little green frogs and one ugly little green frog who are looking for husbands."

"I'd like to meet them," said Moon.

Otter went to visit the frogs. He told them that Moon was looking for a wife to take back with him to the sky.

"He's handsome," replied one frog.

"I'd love to live in the sky and look down on everything," said another.

"My voice would be heard over the entire world," croaked a third.

The ten pretty little green frogs prepared themselves. They put their prettiest combs in their hair. Each one chose a many-colored dress and shiny new beaded shoes. They cooked bowls of roots and pounded sweet seeds into cakes for Moon. Then they climbed into their painted canoes and started rowing toward the other shore.

Little Green Ugly Frog hung her head sadly. Otter asked, ''What's wrong? Don't you want to live in the sky?''

''I didn't think that anyone would want to marry me,'' she answered shyly.

Otter said, ''Moon wants to meet you.'' Little Green Ugly Frog smiled timidly and got ready.

She had no special comb, so she put up her hair as best she could with mud and sticks. She brushed off the tattered old blanket that she always wore and placed green leaves on her feet for moccasins. She had no canoe, so she made a boat from a stick and placed it on the water. Then she broke off a branch for an oar. Little Green Ugly Frog went off to see Moon.

The ten pretty frogs mocked the little ugly one. "You're too ugly to marry Moon! And you don't even have a gift for him."

Little Green Ugly Frog said in a whisper, "I do have a gift, but no one can see it."

The ten frogs laughed even louder. "If it can't be seen, then it doesn't exist."

The ten pretty little green frogs paddled proudly past Moon. They sang and flirted. They looked right at Moon, primping and giggling, and set their cakes and roots on the shore. Moon looked at each and every girl. "They are very pretty," he said to Otter.

Then Moon looked up. In the distance he saw another frog moving toward him. Little Green Ugly Frog, her head bowed, paddled awkwardly in her makeshift canoe. As she placed her oar in the water, wildflowers burst into blossoms on the shore. And in the water Moon saw hundreds of little rainbows.

"How clever," Moon said. "How magical. Whenever she places the branch in the water, things come to life," he marveled.

Moon whispered to Otter, "I'm going to marry Little Green Ugly Frog!"

"Why her?" asked Otter, surprised.

"She has real beauty. She can bring things to life. She'll make a good wife," answered Moon.

As Little Green Ugly Frog paddled closer to Moon, he bent toward her and said, "You are truly beautiful. Will you be my bride and live with me in the sky?"

The frog blushed. She agreed to marry Moon.

Then she rowed home to get ready for the wedding.

The ten pretty little green frogs were so angry they rowed home in a huff.

Little Green Ugly Frog still had no comb. So she picked wildflowers and placed them around the sticks in her hair. Because she had no new dress, she turned her old blanket around so the holes went down the back. She wrapped her feet in red blossoms, broke off a new oar for the canoe, and started the journey to the other shore.

The ten pretty little green frogs were jealous. They lined up by the edge of the beach and waited for Little Green Ugly Frog. As she passed by, they pinched her and scratched her and called her names.

By the time Little Green Ugly Frog reached Moon, she was crying and bleeding and covered with mud. Moon felt sad for her, but despite her appearance he saw only her beauty. He lifted her gently out of the canoe, took magic cornmeal from his pocket, and sprinkled it on her skin to heal her.

For the wedding Moon presented Frog with a beautiful new blanket,
and Otter and his wife gave her a silver comb carved with scallops and
pink shrimps. Frog promised to share her power with Moon in the sky.
Then Moon placed Frog in his heart for their journey to the sky.

Before Moon and Frog left the earth, Moon said to Otter, "Now I will always live in the sky. But you can see me every night." Otter promised to wave to him. And they said good-bye.

That very night Otter saw Moon in the sky with his new wife by his side. When Otter waved, Frog nodded, and the comb in her hair made a silver path of light on the water.

Laughing, Otter dived into the moonlight and swam. Every night Moon and Otter watched for each other.

Frog liked her new home. Moon was a good husband. But when the grizzly bear clouds saw Moon with a wife, they grew envious and once again started chewing on him. Moon grew smaller and smaller and nearly disappeared. Otter searched the sky all night. He feared that his friend was gone forever. Otter wept. Had he lost his friend?

But Frog shared her power. She sang her sacred songs, her heart beating like a drum, and then she swayed back and forth in a magic dance, and just as Moon was about to vanish, her power brought him slowly to full size again.

Since that day Otter sits on the rocks at sunset and waits for Moon. He and his wife and their children still wave. And when Frog nods back, her comb creates the path of moonlight.

And as for those bigmouthed grizzly bear clouds, they are still chewing on Moon. Every month he gets smaller and smaller. But Frog brings him back to full size. It's been happening like that since the earliest times. It will always be that way.

If you look in the sky on a night with a full moon, you can see Frog with her beaded blanket and the shining silver comb that Otter gave her for her wedding.